Property
of Bibi
Family!

Frog and Toad Are Friends

Story and pictures
by ARNOLD LOBEL

SCHOLASTIC INC.

New York Toronto London Auckland Sydney
Mexico City New Delhi Hong Kong Buenos Aires

For Barbara Borack

I Can Read Book® is a registered trademark of HarperCollins Publishers Inc. All Rights Reserved.

Copyright © 1970 by Arnold Lobel. All rights reserved. Published by Scholastic Inc., 557 Broadway, New York, NY 10012, by arrangement with HarperCollins Publishers. SCHOLASTIC and associated logos are trademarks and/or registered trademarks of Scholastic Inc.

ISBN 0-439-45272-4

12 11 10 9 8 7 6 5 4 3 2 1   2 3 4 5 6 7/0

Printed in the U.S.A.

Contents

Spring

Frog ran up the path
to Toad's house.
He knocked on the front door.
There was no answer.
"Toad, Toad," shouted Frog,
"wake up. It is spring!"

"Blah," said a voice
from inside the house.

"Toad! Toad!" cried Frog.

"The sun is shining!
The snow is melting. Wake up!"

"I am not here," said the voice.

Frog walked into the house.
It was dark.
All the shutters were closed.
"Toad, where are you?" called Frog.

"Go away," said the voice
from a corner of the room.
Toad was lying in bed.

He had pulled all the covers
over his head.
Frog pushed Toad out of bed.
He pushed him out of the house
and onto the front porch.

Toad blinked in the bright sun.
"Help!" said Toad.
"I cannot see anything."

"Don't be silly," said Frog.
"What you see
is the clear warm light of April.
And it means
that we can begin
a whole new year together, Toad.
Think of it," said Frog.
"We will skip through the meadows
and run through the woods
and swim in the river.
In the evenings we will sit
right here on this front porch
and count the stars."

"You can count them, Frog,"
said Toad. "I will be too tired.
I am going back to bed."

Toad went back into the house.
He got into the bed
and pulled the covers
over his head again.

"But, Toad," cried Frog,
"you will miss all the fun!"

"Listen, Frog," said Toad.
"How long have I been asleep?"

"You have been asleep
since November," said Frog.

"Well then," said Toad,
"a little more sleep
will not hurt me.
Come back again and wake me up
at about half past May.
Good night, Frog."

"But, Toad," said Frog,
"I will be lonely until then."

Toad did not answer.
He had fallen asleep.
Frog looked at Toad's calendar.
The November page was still on top.
Frog tore off the November page.

He tore off the December page.
And the January page,
the February page,
and the March page.
He came to the April page.
Frog tore off the April page too.

Then Frog ran back to Toad's bed.
"Toad, Toad, wake up. It is May now."

"What?" said Toad.
"Can it be May so soon?"

"Yes," said Frog.
"Look at your calendar."

Toad looked at the calendar.
The May page was on top.

"Why, it *is* May!" said Toad
as he climbed out of bed.
Then he and Frog
ran outside
to see how the world
was looking in the spring.

The Story

One day in summer
Frog was not feeling well.

Toad said, "Frog,
you are looking quite green."

"But I always look green,"
said Frog. "I am a frog."

"Today you look very green
even for a frog," said Toad.
"Get into my bed and rest."

Toad made Frog a cup of hot tea.
Frog drank the tea, and then he said,
"Tell me a story while I am resting."

"All right," said Toad.
"Let me think of a story to tell you."
Toad thought and thought.
But he could not think of a story
to tell Frog.

"I will go out on the front porch
and walk up and down," said Toad.
"Perhaps that will help me
to think of a story."
Toad walked up and down
on the porch for a long time.
But he could not think of a story
to tell Frog.

Then Toad went into the house
and stood on his head.

"Why are you standing
on your head?" asked Frog.

"I hope that if I stand on my head,
it will help me
to think of a story," said Toad.

Toad stood on his head
for a long time.
But he could not think
of a story to tell Frog.

Then Toad poured a glass of water
over his head.

"Why are you pouring water
over your head?" asked Frog.

"I hope that if I pour water
over my head,
it will help me to think
of a story," said Toad.
Toad poured many glasses of water
over his head.
But he could not think
of a story to tell Frog.

Then Toad began
to bang his head
against the wall.

"Why are you banging your head
against the wall?" asked Frog.

"I hope that if I bang my head
against the wall hard enough,
it will help me to think of a story,"
said Toad.

"I am feeling much better now, Toad,"
said Frog. "I do not think
I need a story anymore."

"Then you get out of bed
and let me get into it," said Toad,
"because now I feel terrible."

Frog said, "Would you like me
to tell you a story, Toad?"

"Yes," said Toad, "if you know one."

"Once upon a time," said Frog,
"there were two good friends,
a frog and a toad.
The frog was not feeling well.
He asked his friend the toad
to tell him a story.
The toad could not think of a story.
He walked up and down on the porch,
but he could not think of a story.
He stood on his head,
but he could not think of a story.
He poured water over his head,
but he could not think of a story.

He banged his head against the wall,
but he still could not think
of a story.
Then the toad did not feel so well,
and the frog was feeling better.
So the toad went to bed
and the frog got up
and told him a story.
The end.
How was that,
Toad?" said Frog.

But Toad did not answer.
He had fallen asleep.

A Lost Button

Toad and Frog
went for a long walk.
They walked across
a large meadow.
They walked in the woods.
They walked along the river.
At last they went back home
to Toad's house.
"Oh, drat," said Toad.

"Not only do my feet hurt,
but I have lost
one of the buttons on my jacket."

"Don't worry," said Frog.
"We will go back
to all the places where we walked.
We will soon find your button."
They walked back to the large meadow.
They began to look for the button
in the tall grass.

"Here is your button!" cried Frog.

"That is not my button," said Toad.
"That button is black.
My button was white."
Toad put the black button
in his pocket.

A sparrow flew down.

"Excuse me," said the sparrow.

"Did you lose a button? I found one."

"That is not my button," said Toad.

"That button has two holes.

My button had four holes."

Toad put the button with two holes
in his pocket.

They went back to the woods
and looked on the dark paths.
"Here is your button," said Frog.

"That is not my button," cried Toad.
"That button is small.
My button was big."
Toad put the small button
in his pocket.

A raccoon came out from behind a tree.
"I heard that you were looking
for a button," he said.
"Here is one that I just found."

"That is not my button!" wailed Toad.
"That button is square.
My button was round."
Toad put the square button
in his pocket.

Frog and Toad went back to the river.
They looked for the button
in the mud.
"Here is your button," said Frog.

"That is not my button!" shouted Toad.
"That button is thin.
My button was thick."

Toad put the thin button
in his pocket. He was very angry.
He jumped up and down
and screamed,
"The whole world
is covered with buttons,
and not one of them is mine!"

Toad ran home and slammed the door.
There, on the floor,
he saw his white, four-holed,
big, round, thick button.
"Oh," said Toad.
"It was here all the time.
What a lot of trouble
I have made for Frog."

Toad took all of the buttons
out of his pocket.
He took his sewing box
down from the shelf.
Toad sewed the buttons
all over his jacket.

The next day Toad gave
his jacket to Frog.
Frog thought that it was beautiful.
He put it on and jumped for joy.
None of the buttons fell off.
Toad had sewed them on very well.

A Swim

Toad and Frog
went down to the river.
"What a day for a swim," said Frog.

"Yes," said Toad.
"I will go behind these rocks
and put on my bathing suit."

"I don't wear a bathing suit,"
said Frog.

"Well, I do," said Toad.

"After I put on my bathing suit,
you must not look at me
until I get into the water."

"Why not?"
asked Frog.

"Because I look funny
in my bathing suit.
That is why," said Toad.

Frog closed his eyes when Toad
came out from behind the rocks.
Toad was wearing his bathing suit.
"Don't peek," he said.

Frog and Toad jumped
into the water.
They swam all afternoon.
Frog swam fast
and made big splashes.
Toad swam slowly
and made smaller splashes.

A turtle came along the riverbank.
"Frog, tell that turtle
to go away," said Toad.
"I do not want him to see me
in my bathing suit
when I come out of the river."

Frog swam over to the turtle.

"Turtle," said Frog,
"you will have to go away."

"Why should I?" asked the turtle.

"Because Toad thinks that
he looks funny in his bathing suit,
and he does not want you to see him,"
said Frog.

Some lizards were sitting nearby.
"Does Toad really look funny
in his bathing suit?" they asked.

A snake crawled out of the grass.
"If Toad looks funny
in his bathing suit," said the snake,
"then I, for one, want to see him."

"We want to see him too,"
said two dragonflies.

"Me too," said a field mouse.
"I have not seen anything funny
in a long time."

Frog swam back to Toad.
"I am sorry, Toad," he said. "Everyone
wants to see how you will look."

"Then I will stay right here
until they go away," said Toad.

The turtle and the lizards
and the snake and the dragonflies
and the field mouse
all sat on the riverbank.
They waited for Toad to come
out of the water.

"Please," cried Frog, "please go away!"
But no one went away.

Toad was getting colder and colder.
He was beginning to shiver and sneeze.
"I will have to come out of the water,"
said Toad. "I am catching a cold."

Toad climbed
out of the river.
The water dripped
out of his bathing suit
and down onto his feet.

The turtle laughed.
The lizards laughed.
The snake laughed.
The field mouse laughed,
and Frog laughed.

"What are you laughing at, Frog?"
said Toad.

"I am laughing at you, Toad,"
said Frog,
"because you *do* look funny
in your bathing suit."

"Of course I do," said Toad.
Then he picked up his clothes
and went home.

The Letter

Toad was sitting on his front porch.
Frog came along and said,
"What is the matter, Toad?
You are looking sad."

"Yes," said Toad.
"This is my sad time of day.
It is the time
when I wait for the mail to come.
It always makes me very unhappy."

"Why is that?" asked Frog.

"Because I never get any mail,"
said Toad.

"Not ever?" asked Frog.

"No, never," said Toad.
"No one has ever sent me a letter.
Every day my mailbox is empty.
That is why waiting for the mail
is a sad time for me."

Frog and Toad sat on the porch,
feeling sad together.

Then Frog said,
"I have to go home now, Toad.
There is something that I must do."
Frog hurried home.

He found a pencil
and a piece of paper.
He wrote on the paper.

He put the paper in an envelope.
On the envelope he wrote
"A LETTER FOR TOAD."
Frog ran out of his house.
He saw a snail that he knew.
"Snail," said Frog, "please take
this letter to Toad's house
and put it in his mailbox."

"Sure," said the snail. "Right away."

Then Frog ran back to Toad's house.
Toad was in bed, taking a nap.
"Toad," said Frog,
"I think you should get up
and wait for the mail some more."

"No," said Toad,
"I am tired of waiting for the mail."

Frog looked out of the window
at Toad's mailbox.
The snail was not there yet.
"Toad," said Frog, "you never know
when someone may send you a letter."

"No, no," said Toad. "I do not think
anyone will ever send me a letter."

Frog looked out of the window.
The snail was not there yet.
"But, Toad," said Frog,
"someone may send you a letter today."

"Don't be silly," said Toad.
"No one has ever sent me
a letter before, and no one
will send me a letter today."

Frog looked out of the window.
The snail was still not there.

"Frog, why do you keep looking
out of the window?" asked Toad.

"Because now I am waiting
for the mail," said Frog.

"But there will not be any," said Toad.

"Oh, yes there will," said Frog,
"because I have sent you a letter."

"You have?" said Toad.
"What did you write in the letter?"

Frog said, "I wrote
'Dear Toad, I am glad
that you are my best friend.
Your best friend, Frog.'"

"Oh," said Toad,
"that makes a very good letter."
Then Frog and Toad went out
onto the front porch
to wait for the mail.
They sat there,
feeling happy together.

Frog and Toad waited a long time.
Four days later
the snail got to Toad's house
and gave him the letter from Frog.
Toad was very pleased to have it.